Horse Gone Silent

Shane Ledyard

Self-Published by Shane Ledyard

First Paperback Edition: December 2015

The characters and events portrayed in this book are fictitious. Any similarity to real persons, living or dead, is coincidental and not intended by the author.

Ledyard, Shane, 1976-

Horse Gone Silent: a novella / by Shane Ledyard-1st edition

Summary: Champion show jumping horse Calebo delivers a divinely critical message of hope to the reader in his inspirational tale of perseverance and courage. The story follows the horse's life from the top of his sport to being moments from death by slaughter. Never sure of his ultimate fate, Calebo relies on his faith to give him strength on his incredible journey.

ISBN 978-0692604106 (Paperback)

Printed in the United States of America

For my friend Laura who always does right by the horses.

This book is dedicated to my wife Carice, daughter Kaydy and son Kevin- the best editor a Dad could hope for.
To my mother Kay for her understanding, love, and the encouraging talks at the kitchen table that helped shape me into who I am today.

CONTENTS

"Be alert and of sober mind. Your enemy the devil prowls around like a roaring lion looking for someone to devour."
~1 Peter 5:8

Chapter 1
I Am Not a Baby

Life as a foal was simple. When I was about six months old, everyday my routine was pretty much the same, just like a child may have a set routine when they are growing up. At night I would stay in the barn with my mother and the other mares and foals, while during the day we lived on a forty acre hillside filled with lush, sweet grass. I loved the night time most of all. Our stalls in the barn were bedded thick with straw to protect us from the rubber mats that lined the damp, concrete barn floor. Throughout the night all of us would chew on the golden hay that was piled up loosely in the corner of the stall. Sometimes we would lie down in the bed of straw to rest our growing legs that had been strengthened by grazing up and down the hillsides of the Netherlands during the day. While I lay there, my mother would look down at me, her eyes half open, oozing with a motherly approval. I could feel her love in every look that she gave me. We would talk at night and she would give me advice and encouragement. She would tell me that she believed that I was destined for great things in my life. I loved it when she would do that. It made me feel so important, and filled me with a sense of purpose and anticipation for the future.

Every morning, the barn workers would come in and take us out of our stalls and out to the pasture where we would get to eat grass and play all day with our friends. We would play so many wonderful games together. We learned how to rear, jump, run and how to stay balanced on turns. Turns were important because most of us were bred to become competitive show jumpers, and the better we turned, the more likely we were to win. We all wanted to be winners one day. We were taught that if we won we would bring glory to our blood lines and our parents. That was the first big lie in my life that took me years to uncover. The river, as it were, ran much deeper than that.

In the morning when the barn workers would come and put us out to pasture they would talk amongst themselves. One boy, named Adam, would always come into the stall, slip my halter quietly over my head and say something really condescending like "This is such a cute baby."

I hated it when he would say things like that. My name was Bravado, and my name had meaning. It did at the time anyway. Later on I would actually become known as Calebo, but that was a much scarier and complex time in my life.

I know the boy didn't realize it, but his habit was so incredibly annoying to me at the time. I can understand everything people say-*everything*. I have emotions and feelings just like people. I know how it is to feel love and I know how it is to be deeply hurt. I know anger, jealousy, empathy, happiness and bliss.

To get revenge on the boy for his 'baby' comments sometimes I would step on his foot just enough to get his attention. Or, if I was feeling especially naughty, I would pretend to spook at something knowing full well it would scare him. One day, just for the sport of it, I broke loose from him and ran around the farm. He looked on in horror as I galloped by him at least a dozen times as he stood paralyzed in panic, no doubt full of fear that his boss was going to scold him or perhaps even fire him for the mishap.

Once I felt like he got the message, I trotted over to him and gorged on the handful of grain that he was holding in a bucket that he used to lure me back to him. He stood there watching my sides heave from the self-inflicted workout I had just enjoyed. Sweat started to seep from my neck in the form of a white lather, creating a cloud like pattern against the black hair of my summer coat. Knowing that I was a prized stallion and show jumping prospect, he quickly surveyed my body for any damage. He started his inspection with my four black hooves, then panned upward to each of my white legs that tapered perfectly up to my body which was now underscored by thousands of tiny veins rushing blood to the surface of my ebony body. In the last bite, I took my nose and slammed it up to the back of the bucket, sending it directly into the boy's nose, causing him to slightly tear up. In that moment I felt a touch of guilt but quickly remembered his trite description of me. The guilt vanished quickly as I thought to myself with pride emanating out of my steaming pores, "I am *not* a baby."

Chapter 2
Drunk on a Plane

I can remember the night that my mom tried to warn me about us getting separated. I was lying down in the stall after just eating my dinner. She reached down and let the steam from her warm, moist nostrils lay softly on my cheek.

"Honey, I love you so much," she whispered, her voice shaking with each word that came from her soft lips. "There's something that I need to tell you."

"What is it Mama?" I replied, a lump slowly starting to form in the back of my throat, instinctively reacting to her forlorn tone.

"You see son, there is a time that every colt needs to be separated from his mom."

"What do you mean Mama?" I asked.

"I mean that one day you are going to have to leave my side. It's going to happen suddenly, and it is going to hurt terribly, no matter how much we try to prepare for it. I just want you to know how much I love you and how much I believe in you."

The lump in my throat swelled as tears pushed slowly from my eyes making a zigzag pattern down the hair on my cheeks. "What do you mean Mama? What do you mean?" I asked.

She nuzzled even closer to me this time, her tears starting to mesh with mine, matting the hair on the left side of my face in the pattern of a heart.

"You have a purpose son, a divine purpose and a reason that you are alive. It's not always going to be easy but I know that you are capable of going through this life with confidence. I know you're going to be a leader and make a huge difference in the people around you. My hope for you is that you are surrounded by people that encourage you. In turn I hope you are able to lift others up and help them find their way when they are lost. It's going to take courage, Bravado. Just remember my words, and if you are ever unsure just look inside yourself, and you will find you have everything you need."

"Okay Mama, okay," I replied with the bravest tone that I could use to cover the fear in my voice. We stood together in silence, savoring our time together, both with a sense of loss for a loss that hadn't even occurred yet. As the night wore on we both finally fell asleep, our hearts both tired from bracing against the future.

I have heard it said that people will block things out of their mind that traumatized them when they were young. I wish I could say that I could do the same thing. The day I got taken from my mother is a day I'll never forget. They call it 'weaning', and it is an awful experience that, in the end, makes your body feel like one big useless tear drop that has fallen from one's eye and into the dirt, forming a pool of water that was once part of something whole and pure.

The process was a simple one. They led my mother out of our stall first and took her to our normal field. Then, without warning they took me to another part of the farm where I couldn't see her. I thought at first we were just going to be switching fields. Then, as a few minutes passed I began to worry. I walked the fence line back and forth, my heart rate increasing with each step. Then, encumbered by a pasty morning fog, I heard my mother scream for me. The sound of her voice set me into a frantic gallop. I ran up and down the fence line screaming back, hoping for a glimpse of her. Her screams vacillated between desperation and a motherly attempt to instill some sort of comfort in me.

"You are okay Bravado! Everything is going to be okay. Remember, Bravado, you have a purpose. You have a purpose!"

"Mama! Mama!" I cried.

"It's going to be okay, Bravado. I love you, son, I love you!"

When people say they have no regrets, I say that they haven't lived long enough or they are lying to themselves. I still wish that I had said more to my mom that day, but I just couldn't think of the right thing to say. That was the last time I would ever see my mom.

Shortly afterwards I was moved to a training barn. The next several months I was put into a formal program that almost every riding horse goes through no matter what they end up doing with their career. I was taught about a saddle pad, saddle, girth and the bridle. They showed me how to go around in circles attached to a person standing in the center of the riding ring holding a rope. I would work at the walk, trot and the canter; a process called lunging. The people that I worked with were mostly kind-hearted and did their best to try to help me understand what was going on. They seemed to be taking a lot of time with me on these basic things which I understood quite easily. I started to get a little impatient as I saw the other colts and fillies my age being ridden already. Finally, one day after a lot of work on the circles, the trainers Stefan and Alex put the saddle on me. I was having a hard time catching my breath, and I stood there, panting like a labrador that had just retrieved a duck out of a cold, murky pond. Stefan motioned to Alex with a nod of his head.

"Do you think he's ready Alex?"

"Yes, he's ready," replied Alex. "Let's get on with it."

Alex climbed into the saddle while Stefan held my head still. Alex felt so tense and nervous. He talked like he was so cool about everything but I could tell by the way he clamped his leg against my side that he was afraid that I was going to buck him off. I knew that a lot of horses would do that to riders their first time being ridden. Most of them were underprepared though, and they would just get scared and react with a buck or take off; galloping away out of fear. Alex's fear transcended through his cold, slick leather boots that slid against the hair on my rib cage.

What a chicken, I thought to myself. I considered dropping my shoulder to intimidate him, but then I thought better of it. As that flash of boyish evil crossed my mind, I remembered what my mama had said. She told me to do my best all the time, so I did. I kept my feet on the ground, and did everything that I thought they wanted me to do. Everybody in the main barn had gathered to watch my first ride, and they kept praising me, saying how wonderful I was.

"Oh, he is such a good boy! He is so brave!"

That was some of the easiest praise that I ever received. It did feel good to have people say those things about me. I know now, though, the dangers of working for the affirmation of others, and adjusting who I am based on what I think they want me to be. It just leads to crooked paths and trouble. The praise is nice, but staying true to myself is what I needed to be focused on.

That same night my owner came into the barn, and I overheard him tell the barn manager and the trainer that somebody had bought me. They said that I would be going to the United States. I started to panic because I knew that everybody else who had left to go to the states never came back. I wasn't sure what this meant, but they were acting like it was a big deal, and evidently my owner had sold me for quite a bit of money. His voice was littered with an insatiable combination of greed and temporary satisfaction. As the rancid palpability of his greed filled the room all of the other senses of the barn were flushed out, with the exception of the stench of the manure that had piled up in the corner of each horse's stall. I was going to the states whether I liked it or not. I didn't realize until then that I was just a commodity to him all this time.

Within two weeks of that conversation I was loaded onto a horse van and was in route to the airport. After we got through security, the truck driver drove the trailer directly onto the tarmac. They led me out of the trailer to put me into a portable box that would be picked up and loaded into the plane.

I had never heard all of these sounds before, and the site of the airplanes overwhelmed me, instinctively putting me on high alert. My blood was pumping so fast through my body I could feel my heart strike against the inside of my flesh, pulling my skin back and forth against my rib cage. My tail was straight up in the air as I pranced a few steps across the macadam towards the temporary stall. All I could think about was breaking loose, but I was too afraid to run across the tarmac because all I could see was jet planes and concrete. I blew out of my nose hard in a feral fashion to counter the waft of jet fuel that had seeped into my lungs from the nearby fuel truck. What am I doing here? I thought to myself. Why me?

Frank, the airline assistant who was handling my trip across the Atlantic must have sensed that I was planning on kicking through the portable stall to express my displeasure. He slid a chain across my nose to control me as another person came up behind me and took a small needle and plunged it into the main artery on my neck. Within moments I felt a sensation that I had never felt before. I was completely relaxed in my mind. I lost the desire to kick out or run and I suddenly felt completely in the mood to acquiesce to my captor's requests. Underneath the relaxation was a sickening, dull feeling that something wasn't right. I started to have visions of my dad when he would get paraded past my stall when I was a boy. I saw images of me and my friends playing in the fields, and my mom nuzzling me during those late nights in the stall. It was a myriad of scenes that would elicit sensory emotions that were so clear to me, yet impossible to reflect outside my body. They then put me on the plane where there were other horses, most of them in a similar state as me. The next thing I knew I was in the air. There I was, Bravado-the horse with a purpose; drunk on a plane.

Chapter 3
Get Him Broke

The flight went better than I expected. When we landed, they took me and the other horses to a quarantine facility where I had to spend several weeks to make sure I was free of disease before being introduced to American horses. The people at the quarantine facility treated me very well. However, I had the sense that they were reluctant to get attached. The experience in quarantine felt surreal to me; it was kind of like an orphanage for horses. We all knew that this was just a brief stop in our lives, but we had no idea where we were going to end up. The fluorescent lights in the stalls and aisle ways gave a cold, medicinal feel that matched the aroma of the sanitized environment provided by the caring staff.

Every horse there had been taken away from everything that they ever knew. Our friends and family, the food that we were used to and our routines were all gone. We were thousands of miles away from what we considered life. As a person, you may see hope in that there would be a way you could get yourself back across an ocean. When you are a horse you realize that there's nothing that you can do about your circumstance. I felt fortunate that I could rely on the advice that my mother and my father had given me. I'm very grateful for the way that they treated me and for the things they planted in my heart early on. I knew that not everyone else was fortunate enough to get the same advice, and that was evident in the horses around me at that time.

The quarantine center may have been protecting the world from disease, but so many of the horses there were already contaminated with the disease of anger and fear. Just like people, when horses have fear they don't always show it as such. Fear is an emotion spawned from the devil, and is often the root cause of people and horses morally unraveling into a jaded version of their childhood self. This happens because fear attacks the ego. When one's ego is threatened, it bequeaths upon its host the emotion of anger to cover up for the weakness of fear. This unfortunately is one of the most basic human and equine conditions that is horribly unavoidable in this life. The trouble is that people don't have a level of consciousness high enough to catch themselves before they lash out. One horse I met named Fox Clover was particularly afflicted with this condition of negativity, and he held onto it by choice. He would lament about his life back home, and kept telling me how he couldn't wait until the first American sat on his back so he could drop his shoulder, spin and put them in the dirt. I told him I didn't think that was a good idea and how my mother had taught me that I should always protect my owners and the people that were riding me. He didn't seem to care.

"You know they just pushed me through the baby mill like everybody else. You think that I'm going to reward them by being kind and letting them ride me? No way. You can keep your mama's advice. That's not going to happen. I will be putting them all right where they belong. I will be putting them right in the dirt."

I didn't reply to him. I just turned away and kept eating my hay trying to imagine what life was going to be like for Fox Clover. At that point in my life I couldn't imagine feeling that way about anyone. There would come a time where I could easily relate to him.

The shipper came to pick me up at the quarantine center when my time there was through. I said my goodbyes to everybody that I had met. The young woman named Jill who had looked after me almost every day surprised me when she slipped a peppermint under my chin when she came to greet me in the stall for the last time.

I shifted my upper and lower lip back and forth quickly across her palm to feel for the small, round candy. I wanted to be careful not to bite her. I could smell the dab of perfume that she had put on her wrist that morning for the barn manager that she had a crush on. That pungent, intentional smell mixed with the peppermint in the strangest of ways, reminding me of my old barn in the Netherlands.

Suddenly my mind flashed back, and there I stood right next to my mother. In that moment I was safe, confident and happy. Happy in a way only a boy can be happy when he is with his mom when everything is right. I grabbed the peppermint between my upper and lower jaw carefully and cracked it open. The taste of the mint spread quickly across my tongue and onto the roof of my mouth. I paused momentarily before I went out of the stall. I took a deep sigh and lifted my head to demonstrate some type of courage before I walked straight for the trailer.

Jill handed me off to a man named Tim. He seemed very excited to see me and he told Jill that he had bought me sight unseen and that he believed that I was going to be a Grand Prix show jumper. I suddenly felt a little uneasy because I realized what his expectations were going to be. I remembered the boys back home talking about the Grand Prix classes in America. They spoke of the glamour, the way the horses are put on a pedestal and how they are cared for by an entire team of people. They said each Grand Prix horse, because they jump faster and higher than any other horse in the world are assigned their own veterinarian, groom, rider and trainer. They get to travel the country, jump insanely challenging courses built by the elite course designers of the sport, all in front of huge crowds of people that cheer for us. They also spoke of how difficult it is and how only the best make it. Tim went on to tell Jill how I was going to be a breeding stallion one day as well, as long as everything worked out.

Their words raced through my head. Could I really be a breeding stallion like my dad? A Grand

Prix show jumper? How could I possibly do all this and what if I let them down? This was a lot of information in a very short amount of time for me. I started to feel warm and I broke into a little bit of a sweat. They led me to the trailer, and with all of these thoughts going through my mind it was hard for me to concentrate on what I was doing. Distracted, I caught my toe at the bottom of the ramp and went down on my knees. Tim jerked the metal shank across my nose hard in an effort to pull me back up. Jill gasped in fear that I would be hurt in that brief moment, but fortunately she had wrapped my legs with thick quilt bandages to protect my legs during the trailer ride. After I rebalanced myself, I looked in the trailer, but it was hard to see where I was going with the sun glare coming through the windows. I couldn't really tell where I was walking so I put my head up to let them know of my uncertainty, and the words flashed quickly through my head again; Grand Prix show jumper, breeding stallion. Can I really do this?

I got more nervous and I started swinging my hind end side to side. Tim and Jill got anxious too, perhaps a little annoyed. The tension was building. "You've got to be kidding me, this thing walked onto a plane and flew across the ocean but he won't walk onto my horse trailer? What am I going to tell Bill?" Tim queried out loud, not really expecting a response from Jill.

"Who is Bill?" Jill inquired, trying to settle Tim down by drenching her tone with sympathy.

"He's my financial backer. He is paying for this horse and all his expenses so that I can compete him. He owns Babylon Stables in Colorado where this horse is going. That is if he ever actually gets on the stupid truck!"

When Tim raised his voice I got confused, and then I started getting scared. Finally, Jill, not nearly as emotionally vested as Tim was, spoke up. "Do you mind if I try loading him by myself? I see this almost every week."

"Yea," said Tim, "knock yourself out. I am in no mood to deal with it. I didn't get done at the horse show until super late yesterday and I am not my best. I hate to start off on the wrong foot with him."

Jill took the metal chain shank off of my nose. She clipped the shank to the bottom of my halter so that all I could feel was the sheepskin of the special shipping halter against my nose. I took a deep breath and I relaxed. Jill took a peppermint out of her pocket and crinkled the paper to get my attention. She rolled her shoulders and looked away from me, creating a motion that instinctively said 'follow me'. I stretched my nose down and took a step toward Jill. Tim made an encouraging 'cluck' noise behind my back and I followed Jill onto the trailer. After the longest trailer ride of my life I arrived safely at Babylon Stables.

There was a mare down the aisle way from my stall that I met on my way in. Her name was Brielle. She was a beautiful Hanoverian bred mare with a liver chestnut coat that shined so brightly it looked like it had been drenched with oil. She had huge doe eyes like a white tail deer, and a long slender mouth that curved softly upward toward her large, perfectly cut cheek bones. I thought how lovely she was when I first saw her. Then I noticed something beyond the lovely that I had never felt before. The sight of her sent me to a warm, splendorous state that made me uneasy, a little nervous and overly protective of her all in one moment.

They shut the barn lights off for the night. Just like the quarantine farm they used deep, thin sawdust to bed the stalls. It was such an odd smell to me. I would go as far to call it a cold, stale smell; nothing like the warm scent of the straw that I slept on when I was growing up. I was so tired that I decided to lie down on the first night at my new farm. The sawdust stuck to my hair and caused me to itch, but it was deep and soft nevertheless. It was definitely something that I had to get used to. I tried to shut my eyes to sleep, but found myself waking up every few minutes to make sure that I was okay and to process my surroundings. I didn't have much to say to any of the other horses that night, but despite that, they were all very friendly and welcoming, especially Brielle.

I was awakened by the sound of everyone whinnying and some horses banging their legs against the stall wall. Two men speaking Spanish were in the barn. One of them would stop systematically at each stall and drop two big laps of hay into each metal hay rack in the corner of our stalls. I was so hungry I went right to the corner to get the hay but most of the other horses kept peering through their bars. Some would turn their heads sideways and grab the stall bars with their teeth, running them up and down making the most pernicious of sounds. Feeding time at every barn was noisy, but this place was particularly loud. The second man dumped my grain into my corner feeder. The grain was thick, heavy and syrupy sweet. I could see why everybody was making such a big deal about feeding time. In the middle of my breakfast Tim appeared in front of my stall with a man who I would later find out was his financial backer, Bill. He was the one who spent the money to purchase me and ship me here in the hope that I would become an international star in show jumping. He seemed kind enough, but was insistent on knowing the plan that Tim had for me. Tim politely ignored his request. "So Bill, what do you think of your new horse?"

"Well he certainly looks the part. How far along is he in his training?"

"Well they told me he was broke to ride, but that's about it," replied Tim.

When they say 'broke' in horse terms that is a remarkably ironic slang term for the word 'trained'.

"When do you plan to get on him?"

"I will lunge him and do ground work most of the week, and if all goes well I will get on him Friday when Stephanie is here to be my ground person."

That week presented no real challenges to me. Tim was careful with me, and went very slowly with my training. I could tell he really wanted me to succeed. Friday came and they led me to the wash stall to get tacked up. They slipped a full cheek snaffle into my mouth just like the one they used when they started me in tack at home. There was a copper piece in the middle of the bit that lay flat against my tongue. When it first hit the surface of my tongue it felt like little crystals were running all over my mouth. I rolled my tongue back and forth quickly to try and recreate the sensation.

They led me out to the indoor arena, and I could sense that Tim was anxious. His assistant Stephanie stood in front of me holding both of the reins. Tim placed the mounting block next to me and carefully swung his leg over my back. I walked off for him courageously as he nodded to Stephanie to let go of the reins so he could walk me around the arena.

"Well does he do anything more than walk?" I heard Bill inquire impatiently from the rail as he watched his investment train for the first time.

Tim urged me into a trot. At the time I thought I was doing really well for a three year old under tack. "He wiggles, he wiggles!" Tim exclaimed in a kid-like manner.

He turned to see Bill's demeanor didn't quite match his own enthusiasm. Not all owners get the horse business the way they should. Bill wasn't a bad man, but he was definitely one that didn't get it.

"What do you mean he wiggles?" Bill asked.

"He just seems kind of all over the place like he doesn't know how to ride in a straight line."

Bill took his hand and rubbed it up and down his lower jaw and drew open his mouth slightly as he looked up and cocked his head. He looked straight at me. "Well Tim, get him broke. We have a lot of cash tied up in him. Get him broke."

The next two years of my life I spent doing a combination of different things to prepare for the Grand Prix. Tim trotted me up and down the rolling hills in Northern Colorado where Babylon was stationed. Four days a week I would do flat work under saddle to prepare me for what I needed to do with my feet between the jumps. Most Mondays I would have a day off, and another day or two in a week I got to do what I loved the most. They would work me over grids; a series of jumps put together to tighten my jumping form. The other jump day I would work over courses. From the very start I loved the challenge of jumping, and it felt very natural to me. There's something about being suspended in the air above a jump. My 1200 pound body becomes momentarily weightless, and in that critical moment when I need to be completely clear of the jump I rip my knees upward north of chin and follow that expression with a quick jerk of my hind legs. On landing I feel a rush of splendor gush through my veins and all I want to do is get back in the air as fast as I can. In the air there is nothing but the moment. No past, future or any of the negativity that goes with either of those false states. The voices in my head stop, the memories are gone; anxious thoughts of the future don't exist. I am in the air. I am completely in that moment.

The affirmation I got from the people when I jumped well was like fuel for me. People would watch, and they would say things about me that made me feel like I was important and loved. I lived for it then, and I realize now what a foolish trap the affirmation game is. When I am working for others it ultimately leads to emptiness. When I was a colt back in Europe, one day my father was in a field caddy-corner to mine. He told me that following the spirit that was put inside me by my Maker is the only way I would ever live up to my full potential. It would be much later in life that I would understand what he meant by this advice. Affirmation was my drug of choice in my youth, but like any other drug, the effects wear off and leave you feeling empty. While affirmation from people I truly love was meaningful to me, I just didn't realize at that point in my life who or what I was ultimately working for.

Tim interspersed a few horse shows into my training where I didn't go to compete but I just went to watch. They said it was good for me to go off of the property with the other horses to get used to the show environment. I automatically fell in love with everything about the shows. There was something about the smell inside of the tents at the big horse shows. It was a very distinct smell; it was warm, mildly artificial because of the plastic material of the tents, and when it mixed with the shavings and the moist grass floor it created an atmosphere like nothing I had ever experienced. One of my favorite things about the away horse shows was night time. There was always so much anticipation about the next day for the horses that were going to compete. In the middle of the night the braiders would show up to braid the manes of the show hunters and equitation mounts. There was one braider whom I particularly cared for named Isabelle. She had great energy, and was the hardest working of all the braiders. She couldn't have been any taller than a grand prix jump, and she definitely needed the step ladder that she had to reach the horse's mane with ease. She was a tough girl, pretty, with a genuine way about her that made a barn a better place to be. Even though she wasn't working on me, she always found a way to manage a peppermint into my feed bin before she left for the night.

I can remember the first time I got to actually compete. They brought me to the ring early in the week and I did one of the low schooling jumper classes. Tim had done such an excellent job preparing me at home that the whole thing came easy to me. The adrenaline kicked in as soon as I heard the start buzzer and lasted all the way back to the barn. When we made our way back to the tents Tim was elated with my performance.

"He was so brave! He was so good!" he said to everyone that would listen.

They made such a big fuss of me and it was the first time that I actually felt like I belonged where I was. Tim handed me off to the groom, Stephanie and then grabbed his phone.

"Who are you in such a hurry to call?" asked one of the junior riders who was getting ready for her class.

"Bill, I have to call Bill"

"Why?" she asked.

"I have to tell him the news. Bravado is broke. And he is going to be a star!"

Chapter 4
The Circuit

I once heard one of my favorite veterinarians describe a Grand Prix horse as a freak of nature. That is what I was-a freak of nature. Jumpers at this level are like any professional athlete at the top of their sport. Capable of jumping jumps over five feet in height with spreads just as daunting; they are the outliers, the abnormal ones, the elite. Fortunately for me, horses at this level are treated very similar to their human counterparts. I had access to the best hay and grain and nutritional supplements on the market. I was treated regularly by a chiropractor, acupuncturist, and massage therapist. The bedding in my stall was banked high against the walls so I could freely roll and not risk damaging my legs. I had a personal groom that massaged my legs after hard works, and rubbed my coat slick to perfection. I traveled all over the country and followed the sun. I was in Colorado in the summers and Florida, Mississippi or California in the winters. In between I showed in great horse show towns like Culpeper, Virginia and Devon, Pennsylvania.

It felt like I was living in a dream. Everyone watched me from the moment I would walk out of the stall. I had grown to just over seventeen hands. With all the attention from my team every time I walked to the ring to compete I looked like a groom walking down the wedding aisle to marry the love of his life. How I savored the attention that I received! I believed this was the purpose that my mother had spoken of, and I was living up to everything that she had ever taught me. At the same time part of me was feeling mysteriously incomplete, like there was something else that I needed to be doing. I pushed it down though. Any emotion that would get in the way of my work was cast aside, allowing me to crystallize my focus on my job. That crystallization combined with my dream-like state was the perfect combination for creating a magnificent illusion of purpose in my young mind.

I wasn't the only one that believed in the horse show product as an end in itself. There are others who held the show jumping illusion close to their heart, but were also missing the whole message. I remember one day in particular where there was a young boy watching me on the rail at a big Grand Prix in Pennsylvania. The big class was held on a Thursday night, very different than my normal Sunday class. It was under the lights that night and we arrived to the warm up ring about 6:30. The sun was just starting to set, and my eyes had to adjust between the lights of the arena and the natural light of the setting sun. I was stretching out at the walk with hundreds of people shoulder to shoulder against the arena fence looking on; all vying for a chance to just watch us warm up.

I had a trademark move that I liked to do when I felt like showing off. I would extend my front hooves forward past my normal footfall, placing them down in a dramatic fashion, the last second cupping my hoof on the freshly groomed footing with an elegant touch. I was in the midst of this routine when I noticed a young man who seemed to take a particular interest in the whole horse show scene. He was a slender boy in his early twenties with ginger hair locked mostly away under a well worn baseball cap. He was standing next to an older woman whom I was pretty certain was his mother. They both had eyes that sparkled bright in the summer dusk; hers for the pride in her son for what she believed was to come of him, and his for his dream of what was to be.

Tim sent me forward with urgency, his formal white breeches in stark contrast with his perfectly polished boots that were just starting to catch the artificial light coming from the grand stand.

We galloped to the base of our first warm up jump of plain white rails, about three and a half feet high and three and a half feet wide.

"Go up two," Tim said to his ground man after each jumping effort.

The rails steadily were raised towards the tape at the top of the standards, indicating our schooling limit. Once I was plenty limber, Tim rode me really deep to a tall vertical, and I rubbed it hard with my front legs.

"That'll do," he said as he steered me towards the in-gate, working me laterally in order to stay stretched out for the class.

As I was finishing my warm up I walked by the boy and his mom one more time, and I heard his mother say to him the same thing that my mom had told me on one of those cold, Netherland nights cuddled deep in my bed of straw.

She held his arm, and reached up and whispered in his ear. "Now don't you worry about a thing, son. You will get your chance, and you are going to be great. You're going to do amazing things."

A tear welled in the boy's eye, and, remembering my own mother's words of encouragement, I followed immediately with my own tear. Then the boy, with a desire so raw it was palatable, leaned down to his frail, but spry mother.

"God I love this," he whispered in her ear.

Just as I stepped into the ring to jump my clear round, those words kept playing over and over again in my mind; God, I love this.

I spent the next several years of my life competing on the circuit. Usually going to the show ring twice a month, I would be given December and August off to rest while turned out at the farm. It was a great lifestyle that I started to take for granted. Being surrounded by the best of the best became a habit for me and my childhood had started to become a distant memory. I thought I was safe in assuming that this is what life was all about. My team seemed happy with me, as I would nearly always be in the ribbons. Every once in a while I'd have a rail down when Tim would sit down a little bit too early in the tack coming off of a wide jump. The weight of his seat would push my hind end down just enough that I would catch a rail with a hind leg and send it bouncing out of the jump cups and to the ground. He was always quick to take the blame, even though I felt like I could try a little harder in that moment.

The years on the circuit had passed by quickly, and as a 13 year old I was slated to have my best year. I overheard Tim telling everybody how he expected this to be the year that I would really put him on the map, proving him to be one of the best riders in the country. I had gotten used to the pressure created by those statements. When I heard Tim say these things it didn't bother me. It actually just got me excited because I believed I would rise to the challenge. I knew I could take care of business. I would wake up on the morning of a show looking forward to that moment in the air when everybody was looking at me and studying every single part of my body while holding their breath; all their hope clinging to the notion that my legs would stay up in the air and clear the rails. I knew in that moment I was the only one that had the control of whether or not we were going to win the class. It was one of the best feelings that I would ever experience in my life.

Poised to help Tim accomplish his career goals and to continue to fulfill my purpose, it was just another day in Babylon where everything was just right. That was until I started to rub the jumps. That year, it just seemed like every time I went to the ring it got harder and harder to leave all the rails in the cups. It started with one rail down, then two, and then three in a class. With the scoring based on time and faults per rail, it was tough to hear the announcer tell the crowd that I had multiple jumping and time faults in a round. That is the equivalent of a baseball player striking out three times in one game. Everybody seems to look at you differently, and nobody has anything very nice to say. I was failing, and I knew it.

I was starting to get a little sore here and there but I didn't think it was a big deal. Then one day I was in the schooling ring and Tim noticed I started drifting right before the jumps to compensate for the pain I was experiencing. I started to get more and more anxious everyday knowing that I couldn't get the job done like I used to. I could tell Tim had lost his faith in me, and that just made things worse because it started to affect my heart.

"He's just not right," he would tell his ground crew and groom. "I don't know what his problem is."

One morning Bill came by to ask Tim what he was going to do about my drop in performance. "Bravado just doesn't seem to want to leave the jumps up anymore and it's starting to get a little embarrassing. He didn't even make the time allowed last week at the show in Chicago."

"I will get him right Bill. He just needs a little time."

Bill was clearly annoyed by his generic answer. "Just do whatever it takes, would you Tim? Do whatever it takes."

Distracted by a text message from his business, Bill broke his eye contact with Tim and walked out of the barn. The atmosphere didn't change even though the source of tension had left. Tim repeated Bill's orders. "Ok, Bravado, you heard the man. We'll do whatever it takes."

Chapter 5
Dead Unicorns

The next few months were brutal as Tim tried to figure out how to get me to jump in my old form. The level of stress started to give me ulcers, and after about twenty minutes into my ride my stomach would be in tremendous pain which made it even harder for me to perform. Tim was doing everything he could, but realized he needed outside help. He called his veterinarian, Dr. Landing.

I saw the doctor's truck pull up and immediately started to worry, which in turn aggravated my stomach. Brielle saw that I was getting stirred up.

"Don't worry, Bravado. Dr. Landing is the best. He will take good care of you."

"Thanks Brielle," I replied, it is just that so much of me hurts and I am afraid that they are going to start injecting my joints."

"Don't sweat the injections, she replied. They are going to knock you out for it and you won't feel a thing. Dr. Landing is a great horseman and he even rides too. Just be sure to stay very still when they go into your joints with the needles."

"Have you ever had the needles?" I asked.

"Every six months since I was nine years old. And truthfully the medicine has helped me and so many other horses extend their careers and become more comfortable. They do it to help you, and it will. It will be okay, I promise."

I reached down and grabbed some hay and quickly looked up with my eyes wide, waiting to see Dr. Landing come down the aisle.

"Thanks again Brielle" I said, half embarrassed that she needed to console me and half elated that she made the effort.

Dr. Landing made his way down to my stall, and asked Tim to pull me out so he could do his work up. He watched me work both directions on the lunge line and had Tim jog me back and forth after flexing all four of my legs, one at a time.

"Tim it looks like he could use his hocks and stifles injected. We should get him on medication for ulcers too since he is so symptomatic. You could have his stomach scoped to be sure, but my guess is he has a belly full of ulcers giving him fits."

"Let's just get after it Doc."

"Okay, Tim. Let's get started."

Brielle belonged to Hailey, one of the junior riders in the barn that rode under Tim. Hailey was there that day with her dad, Thomas who happened to be an expert both in sarcasm and judgment of character. Thomas was a naturally funny man, the type that made you smile just by him being in the room. Very tall and strong, you could tell he genuinely loved his daughter with everything in his heart.

"You brought out the big guns for Bravado, huh?" Thomas quipped as Tim walked by. Tim had spent a lot of time at the shows with Thomas while guiding Hailey through her junior career, so he knew when Thomas was in the mood to bust on him.

Tim just gave a half smile out of the corner of his mouth and rolled his eyes.

Thomas pressed forward with his thoughts as if he had written the lines for a stand-up comedy act before he got to the barn that day. "It's all rainbows and unicorns when you go to buy one of these things until they start to need a little bit of help."

Just then one of the adult amateur riders walked out of the tack room smelling of saddle soap and dried sweat.

"What do you mean by that Thomas-rainbows and unicorns?"

"Well you know, when we get into this sport it just seems like all it is going to be is going to the barn and riding around in circles for an hour."

I could see Tim start to get uncomfortable, but Thomas pressed on with his unwelcomed insights of the inglorious realities of horse showing.

"I just thought my kid would jump some jumps at home, then go to a horse show a couple times a month to win a fifty cent ribbon for the wall."

"Yea, sounds about right Thomas," Tim said dismissively, hoping Thomas would get the hint that he didn't want him to over inform the rest of the barn about the innards of his business.

"It's just not as linear as the cover of the horse magazines suggest. I guess that's the same with any sport though. If someone told me in the beginning that my daughter's horse would need things like a chiropractor and acupuncturist to perform it's best, I don't think I ever would have bought in."

"You are on a bit of a rant here aren't you Thomas?" asked Tim, his tone quietly suggesting that Thomas take it down a notch. His comment was followed by Doc Landing pricking my neck with a chemical cocktail to knock me out for the injections. Suddenly I felt numb, spacey and tired.

"Let me finish, because as much as I joke, in my experience this sport is about a whole lot more than just riding. Just as long as my little girl is safe and keeps smiling-that's all that really matters to me. And some fifty cent ribbons are always nice too."

Their conversation drifted in and out as I tried to stay coherent. I wished they would just be quiet. It is so much better when the people are quiet.

That same night a couple of the other horses in the barn were talking about one of our dear friends who had gone to a horse show the previous week and crashed through a very big jump. Freelander, or "Freely" as we called him, was an amateur's horse. He was competing in one of the divisions late in the day that he had done dozens of times. It was awfully hot, and it was one of the last days of the horse show, leaving him a little more tired than usual. He was coming around the corner of the arena toward a jump and he stared up at the center of the obstacle to line up where he was going to leave from, but just as he was clear on his spot things went horribly wrong. Two dogs started fighting outside the ring. Their ruckus distracted him for a brief moment, and by the time he looked back it was too late. He went chest first through the jump, the hard wooden poles slamming into his body. The force of the blow caused him to recoil back as he scrambled with terror at the rails that were piling up underneath his front feet. He finally broke free, embarrassed from the failure and stricken with fear because he knew he was hurt but he couldn't tell how badly. His rider ended up on the other side of the jump, landing shoulder first with a mouth full of sand and grit, her canary colored breeches christened with stains reflecting the reality of her failed attempt to clear the jump.

The rumor was that Freely was going to be okay and that he would only be out for a month. For some reason though it just seemed to be the way things were going at that time. Fortunately, most of us never have to go through anything like that. Any good horse will tell you that the horse business is filled with people with very big hearts and most horses would agree that people do everything they can to help us and protect us. We love having a purpose and meaning. We love to have a job to do.

Horses also know what we have done for people for hundreds of years before we were used just for sport. We have helped countries win wars by going directly into fierce battles, risking our lives for human conquest and progress. We have traveled over thousands of miles of land to help settle colonies that grew to major cities. We know we are important to our people and we know they do their best by us. Like anything else though, sometimes there are shades of grey.

The plan was to give me a couple of days off after the joint injections and the medications to see how I was. I felt fantastic when they brought me out of my stall for my first day of turn out after just being hand walked the day before. I took off the moment they let me go. I jumped and snorted and bucked with enthusiasm. I could tell that Tim was worried that I would get hurt playing.

"Whoa, Bravado. Whoa boy," he begged as I ripped past the gate. I slowed it to a jog for his benefit, and flipped my tail and snorted fast and loud to be sure everyone saw how good I looked.

Later that week I started back into light work, and within a month I was back at a horse show.

Tim kept saying how well I was jumping in the lower divisions that I had been demoted to since my performance had been suffering. He felt like I had enough to get back to the Grand Prix the following week. Feeling a little pressure from Bill as well, he entered me in the big class at the next competition.

We were headed to Gateway, which was one of the more popular shows, and I knew a lot of my friends were going to be there for the Grand Prix. I got excited when I heard Tim talking about the class, and that excitement was infectious to the rest of the barn. Everyone was talking about my return to the top. Sunday morning Tim came in to the barn already wearing his formal white britches for the class that afternoon. He had a swing in his step and stopped by my stall to slip a mint into my feed bucket. I pushed the sweet red and white striped candy around my plastic bucket which made an odd, hollow scraping sound until I was finally able to grab a hold of it with my teeth. The other horses next to me started to nicker and paw, begging Tim for the same attention. His focus however was entirely on me.

"Okay Bravado. You ready to make this happen today?"

I was really eager to compete and couldn't wait for that afternoon. We went to the schooling ring to get my jumping technique sharpened up. I felt great and I really thought I was using my hind legs better in the air than I had in a long time.

"Are you good?" Tim's ground person asked him just as we cleared our tenth warm up fence.

"Yeah I'm good. Let's go," replied Tim.

Tim was completely in the zone and ready to compete. I felt like we were in for a really good round and it was definitely my kind of jump course. It was set outdoors and it left a lot of room to gallop, perfect for a horse like me with a huge stride. There was nothing about it that even remotely intimidated me.

The first jump on course was a big gray vertical designed to blend in with the background of the arena. It didn't offer any challenge to me and we galloped on in a very smooth seven strides to a wide blue oxer. We turned right, passed the in-gate and Tim steered me back to the center of the arena to a combination of jumps with two strides in between them. I jumped the vertical at the entry of the combination excellent, but landed awkward and caught my front toe in a clump of deep footing. This forced me to get to the oxer element a little too late. Desperate, I pushed extra hard off my right hind leg, and when I did I felt something wasn't right in my left hind leg. We barely made it over the oxer and as soon as I landed, I yanked my hind leg up as high as I could to my belly to take the pressure off the injured limb. Tim quickly pulled me up to a stop. I walked out of the ring gingerly, and the team got me back to the stall and immediately called the veterinarian. One of the grooms took ice cold water and hosed my leg until the vet showed up.

Dr. Landing and Tim hardly spoke. Dr. Landing asked Tim to walk me a few steps but I limped so bad he immediately told him to stop. He quickly walked to his truck and drew a painkiller up for me in a syringe. I stood still as he plunged the needle into my neck. I almost immediately felt better with the drugs in me, but at the same time I knew something was definitely wrong. I had never seen Tim so solemn.

Dr. Landing got his ultrasound machine and proceeded to investigate the interior of my leg. The tool he used felt very queer against my leg as the doctor tried to find evidence of damage. I couldn't see entirely what was happening but what I could see was the look on Tim's face when the doctor pointed towards the portable ultrasound screen. Dr. Landing shook his head side to side with an empathetic fashion that I had never seen from him before.

Tim looked at me and then quickly looked away. In a flash of violence that I had never seen from him before he pushed a pile of hay over that was stacked nearby, and followed up by kicking a feed bucket across the barn aisle. Tim kept walking to go cool off and Stephanie put me back in my stall where I waited for the effect of the sedation to wear off.

They calculated that I would need an entire year to rest before I could even consider going back to work. As they had done so many times before, Tim and Bill stood in front of my stall to discuss my future. At that point, I don't think that Tim had come to grips with what had happened in the ring that day. I could tell he was blaming himself and I wish that I could tell him that he had done absolutely nothing wrong. He had always been such a great rider and trainer. I knew his heart was in the right place. He didn't realize that there was a soft spot in the footing that day causing me to stumble. I remember wishing that I could take him back to that ring and show him myself so that it would ease the burden of guilt that he was putting on himself.

“Well Bill, Tim asked, “what do you want to do with him?”

“We kept him a stallion for a reason. It’s time he goes to the breeding barn. It's time to make more Bravados.”

Chapter 6
Make More

Springtime came and I was off to the breeding shed. I was raised to be a gentleman so I'm not going to get into too many details about what goes on there. Let's just say that first year was extremely exhausting.

My first crop of babies that year yielded two colts and five fillies. A stallion often times will never get to meet his children unless they happen to be raised at the same farm where he lives. I was fortunate that they decided to leave my first born son Whiskers at the farm where I was living. They tried to keep him separate from me as per protocol. Every once in a while though they would lead him by my stall close enough where he would quickly pull the lead rope through his handler's hand and put his nose to mine. We would quickly say hello as our nose's touched, and I would give him a quick nod of approval before his handler would give him a corrective growl and yank his head back straight.

In my second year on the breeding farm, my prayers were answered when they actually started turning Whiskers out in the field next to mine. I would get to watch him run and play with the other young colts just like I used to do. When he would get tired he would come over and stand by me under a huge old sycamore tree. The branches from the antiquated tree spread over both of our fields, providing shade from the early spring sun.

He asked me about everything. The circuit, what it was like to be on a plane, and most importantly to him, he wanted to know what it was like to win. It meant so much to have somebody to talk to and to give advice to. He was always so eager to please me.

"Daddy, one day I want to be a show jumper too," he would say to me, his eyes wide open with hopeful expectancy of my affirmation.

I hoped and I prayed that he would have the same opportunities that I did, and that he would have a rider like Tim. It hurt my heart so much the day that I had to leave him, but something unexpected was about to happen again in my life.

It had rained terribly for several days straight so they didn't turn any of the horses outside to graze. Everybody was eager to get out and I was no exception. Whenever I would get locked up for that amount of time I would start to lose my mind.

Once the rain finally stopped, they started to lead us out, one by one. When the barn manager Jennifer came into my stall I could hardly keep my feet on the ground. An experienced handler, she recognized that I was fresh and she slowly weaved the metal chain shank over my nose in order to get more control. She led me out the stall, and I was so full of energy that I almost pushed her over on my way through the door. I danced and jigged sideways my whole way to the paddock. She led me in and turned me around so that I would face the gate. My heart raced, and I sensed Jennifer was anticipating an explosion from me. She slipped my halter off and in order to keep her safe I took a deep breath while waiting for her to step back out of the field. The moment she latched the gate I took off. I felt so good that I ran around the pasture several times in both directions. I twisted and turned my neck and put my head down in between my knees to let out a buck that sent my muscles quivering like an ocean wave from my ears to my tail. I felt like a two year old. Jennifer stood and watched in amazement, and after a suitable display I broke into the trot in a figure eight pattern, snorting and blowing. After about 10 minutes, I settled into a patch of tall, lush grass. Jennifer was talking on her phone while keeping her eyes directly on me. Curious, I walked closer to her so I could hear what she was saying.

"Tim, you are not going to believe this, but I just saw that old Bravado horse trot. Tim, I think he's sound. Actually I know it, he looks completely healed."

"Are you sure Jennifer?"

"Well, you need to come see for yourself. But I am telling you, from what I am seeing the big horse is all right."

"Okay, I will be right over."

That afternoon they put me on a lunge line so they could watch me trot in circles in both directions. They agreed that I was sound, and they had Dr. Landing come and ultrasound my leg to make sure it looked healed from the inside. They put me in my stall and met outside my stall once again to talk about my future.

The discussion was detailed. As it turned out there was such a big influx of talented horses being imported from Europe that breeding in the United States was not considered a profitable venture. That notion, along with the fact that I was healed meant that I was going to be able to compete again. Dr. Landing told Tim that I should probably never jump to the height of the Grand Prix again, but I could certainly be a teacher to people learning how to ride. I knew what that meant. Often times there were younger riders that wanted to learn how to jump and they would need an experienced horse to keep them safe. That all sounded fine, but then came the rub. Because of my sudden career change, I was going to have to be castrated because the junior riders who I was going to teach were not allowed to compete stallions. They discussed that too. This was definitely one of the times that I wished that either I couldn't understand people or that I was able to talk!

A week later the vet came back and sedated me for the procedure. The drugs they gave me felt similar to what I had on the plane but this time I got so weak that I had to lie down on the ground. When I was finally able to get up I was extremely sore. Now, officially a 'gelding', they moved me back to the show barn. I was elated to be able to see Brielle again, but I really missed my son, Whiskers. I would pray for him at night, hoping that I would get to see him again one day. Over the next ninety days they slowly brought me back into training. We did a lot of trail riding which I really enjoyed. This was a new time of my life and it definitely felt like this was where I was supposed to be.

After about seven months Dr. Landing gave the go-ahead for me to start jumping small courses again. Late one afternoon Tim came walking down the barn aisle followed by a tall, slender blonde haired girl. She was wearing a helmet and was very well turned out, as if she had hand picked her clothes out of a catalogue that morning. Her breeches were perfectly clean, and she wore a purple polo shirt tucked in neatly that led to her slim waist accented with a belt made out of bridle leather. Her boots were polished, although barely broke in, and she wore a long spur that didn't seem to match the experience of her newer boots.

"Tiffany, this is Bravado, the horse that your father leased for you to ride," Tim said, motioning toward my stall.

"What do you think?" he continued, clearly expecting the young rider to be impressed by me, and at the same time obviously getting aggravated at her lack of attention.

Tiffany looked up from her phone just long enough to get a glance at me.

"Yeah, he's cute enough I guess. Is somebody going to tack him up?

"Carlos will tack him up for you," Tim replied, doing his best to hold back his disdain for the princess of a girl that was going to be riding his old partner.

"He will be ready in about fifteen minutes."

Chapter 7
I Hate This Horse

My first job in my new role as a teacher was to help Tiffany get to the children's jumper division. An easy enough job by all accounts, I was happy to accept my first challenge after my breeding career.

At first glance I couldn't understand why Tim didn't seem to care for Tiffany, but I quickly figured it out. Tiffany was not like Brielle's rider Hailey, who was brought up so well by her father to be kind, respectful and humble, despite being raised in a privileged fashion. Tiffany was cut from a different cloth. I always liked to give people the benefit of the doubt because sometimes people act a certain way because they have been hurt emotionally in their lives or simply misunderstood. I considered myself to be a patient horse, and gave her as much slack as I could. That was, until she climbed into the tack.

What a wretch! The torment began when she went to mount. She took her toe, and instead of pointing it toward the girth where it wouldn't hurt me, she jabbed me directly in my rib cage. She then proceeded to slam her overly privileged rear end onto my back so hard that the cantle of the saddle dug in to my loins. I scooted to get away from the pain and she subsequently snatched the reins, ramming the bit into the top of my mouth. Evidently she didn't see my look of horror because for some reason she was staring straight down at my neck. She then yanked up on the reins hard to stop me, while she simultaneously rolled her eyes and screamed "whoa!"

The tone of her voice made it clear that she assumed this debacle was entirely my fault. She reseated herself and we went to work at the trot. She sawed the bit back and forth on my mouth without any sign of mercy while she drove her spurs into my sides in an alternating fashion, making it feel like someone had put a drunken Pinocchio on my back.

What is wrong with his girl? I thought to myself, caught in a sudden misery that I never knew was possible.

We went on to the canter, but she wasn't much better at the third gait. She perched herself over the pommel of the saddle, rotating her hips like an overloaded washing machine as she attempted to steer me around the ring. When the ride was through she slid down and pulled the reins over my head. With the stirrups still dangling at my side she tossed the reins to Carlos.

"I hate this horse," she said arrogantly.

Unbelievable. I went from being a famous show jumper, to a breeding stallion, to dealing with this mess of a girl. What a remarkable turn of events. I had no idea at that time that Tiffany would end up being a highlight compared to what was to come in my life.

The arrangement was that she was supposed to lease me for a year to compete me in the children's jumper division. As it turned out, I carted her around the show ring for 6 months when fate intervened and distracted her with a harem of teenaged boys that caused her to lose interest in riding. Her father had enough of her nonsense and paid off the lease early, releasing me from my daily torture.

I thanked God when I heard the news. The next 18 months I was ridden by different riders, all of whom were great kids trying just to learn the ropes of show jumping. My job was to protect them and I took it very seriously. There were many times when I had to jump from really far away from the base of the jump because the riders rode me to a spot where I had no other choice but to leap from about eight feet out. They would grab my mane for balance and grip tightly with their knees in an attempt to stay in the middle of the tack as their parents gasped in horror from the rail. I liked saving the riders when they got in trouble at the jumps. The kids that rode me during that time of my life seemed to be really appreciative of what I was doing for them. From all the talk that I heard up and down the barn aisle, it seemed like this was going to be my lot in life. As long as I didn't run into too many more kids like Tiffany I was comfortable accepting that this was how I would spend the rest of my life.

Then came news that would change life as we knew it at Babylon Stables. The stock market had crashed and the owner of Babylon was going to lose everything, including the horses he was supporting. He was too ashamed to show his face at the barn, so he had Tim stay on to sort through getting all of us placed in new homes. One by one I saw my friends leave, including Brielle. Because she was privately owned, she would stay with

Hailey, which made me happy for her even though I was heartbroken that we would be split apart.

"I am going to miss you Bravado," Brielle told me the night before she was scheduled to be shipped to her new home.

I wished terribly that I could dry her tears for her. The stall bars between us were cold and hard, making the distance down the aisle seem even farther. I wouldn't touch my hay that night as we talked quietly until the morning feeding. Exhausted from the emotions we exchanged, she hung her head as she followed Hailey out of the barn and onto the trailer. We both knew it would likely be the last time we would ever see each other. My heart ached terribly for her.

Everyone was going to different farms, most of which we had heard about while we were on the circuit. As the barn was getting empty of horses, I couldn't understand why I hadn't been placed yet. I thought I was so useful, but evidently the area trainers were hesitant to take a shot at me because they knew about my injury history. There was no fooling anyone because I was so easy to identify with my prominent brand on my flank and the permanent swelling on my leg from my old injury. Everyday I waited anxiously for news of where I would end up. Secretly I hoped I would end up at the same barn with Brielle so we could spend the rest of our lives together, grazing side by side, reminiscing about our lives. That would be a wonderful way to end up. Any horse would be happy with that fate.

It wasn't going to happen that way though. Everyday that I had to wait, I noticed that I got less and less hay and the quality of the care was going downhill. Tim seemed very hollow inside, and he didn't ever say much. Then finally I got the news regarding my destination. Because I was so tolerant of all of the different types of people that had been riding me, they told me I was going to be sent to Thompson Therapeutic Riding Center to help handicapped children learn to ride. The comment made my head spin with doubt. Why on earth would they send me there?

Chapter 8
Casting a Shadow

I really had no idea what I was in for. I was loaded onto a small two horse trailer and transported to my new home a couple hours south. The Thompson barn manager was named Holly, and she carefully took me off the trailer when I arrived. As soon as I backed off the trailer I whipped my head up and around to get a sense of my surroundings. There were several large fields with run-in style sheds, and the horses were turned out in groups together. At first glance, it looked like a barn of misfits, and I was about to become one of them. There were small ponies, a donkey, draft horses and quarter horses. The pedigree of the horses was nothing like the show and breeding barns that I was used to. All the horses picked their heads up from grazing to take a look at the new guy, and then quickly put their heads back down to the grass, keeping one eye on me as I marched toward the barn. When I walked through the barn doors I couldn't believe how many people were excited to see me. I had no idea what I was in for, but I learned quickly that everyone at this barn loved to groom! Immediately I felt loved, and my heart was filled with gratitude.

Different kids would pull me out of the stall, sometimes several times a day to rub on my coat. Everybody was so very generous in their attitude and their heart. In one week I think I got more treats than I ever had in my entire life. In the weeks following they got me used to something called side-walkers which was completely different than anything I had ever experienced before. One person led me while two people would walk on either side of me. This was done because some of the riders needed assistance to stay in the saddle for their therapy. After two weeks of this special preparation and desensitization, the program manager Lindsay approved me for the therapeutic work. It was time to start my new career.

I will never forget my first rider at the therapy program because she did something to my heart that nobody else ever had. I would have thought that the riders in this program would have been depressed or sad because they didn't necessarily have all the faculties that everybody else had around them. That was a very ignorant perspective on my part, and I was ashamed that I thought that way. The day I met Claire, I realized how foolish my thinking was. She came down the barn aisle wearing special braces on her arms to help her walk. Immediately I was drenched with a kind of heart felt humility that I had never experienced. Her smile was radiant with an honest joy, and she instantly made everyone around her better, including me. I had a little bit of a chip on my shoulder coming in to the barn being the big shot Grand Prix horse, and this distasteful self-centered perspective was washed clean in my service to her. Claire helped me realize something extremely important that day. It is purpose, not glory, and service, not comfort that makes a regular horse a great horse and an average person an exceptional individual.

I was so much larger than her at my 17 hands that I cast a shadow over her when she walked over to brush my coat in preparation for the ride. My shadow was drowned out by the light that emanated from her pure spirit. Once I was tacked and ready to go, Claire walked up a special ramp so she could get closer to my back. My handlers put me alongside the ramp very cautiously so that she could climb into the tack. We did a lot of walking, and Claire rode wonderfully, her hips following the rhythm of my walk with a natural ease found only in the best of riders. I could sense her smile in her ride, and when she rode me I felt so free of trouble. I could only hope she felt the same way.

As time went on I got to help so many wonderful children and adults with their riding. Some of the people in the program would canter me while some chose to simply walk. It didn't matter to me what we did because it seemed like no matter what, everybody was always so grateful for the time that they spent with me, and that was all the payment and encouragement that I could hope for. As much as I enjoyed my work at the therapy center, there was a voice deep inside of me telling me that this would not be the last place I would live. The slow, steady riding that the therapy riders needed strengthened me over several months. One day I came out of my stall feeling like I could jump a track of five foot jumps. This feeling created a lot of inner conflict for me because I cared about the riders at Thompson so much. At the same time the athlete in me that God had created was trying to come out, and I sensed that there was more in my life that I had to do. I struggled with this but I never let it interfere with my job because I didn't want to let anybody at the program down.

Then the unthinkable happened again. Word came down the barn aisle that the money ran out for the therapeutic center. They were operating primarily on donations and fundraisers, both of which had run dry in the weak economy. Despite the amazing work that Thompson was doing for the community, there was nothing that anyone could do to help them survive.

A horse dealer of ill repute named Arthur entered the barn one afternoon shortly after we heard the news. Arthur was charming, but charming in that creepy sort of way that made me want to stand in the back of my stall with my tail facing the door. I could hear him talking a line to Holly and Lindsay in an unsettling sort of way that made me sense there was something just not quite right. This shady man was dressed in new jeans, an imitation designer shirt and pointy, roach-killer cowboy boots that had never seen the inside of a stirrup. His hair was too perfect, like he tried harder than he should have to look good. His cheap cologne was mutated to a disastrous odor by the stench of his cigarette stained fingers and the auction-barn egg sandwich on his breath. “Don’t worry Holly, I'll give this one a great home.”

He scanned his wincey brown eyes up and down my body. “How much do you want for him?”

Holly and Lindsay looked at each other. “What do you think Arthur?”

“How about three hundred?”

“No way!” retorted Lindsay, that is even below meat price! What are you planning on doing with him?”

“I told you, I will give him a great home, but I have my costs too.”

Both girls just stared back at him with disdain and mistrust. I could sense their anger which had been accumulating since the loss of the program, and they projected it squarely on the necessary evil standing in front of them.

“Fine, I will give you five hundred.”

The girls reluctantly agreed, biting their lips in a vain effort to hold back their tears. They took me out of my stall one last time and handed me over to my new owner.

I stared sickened at the site of my transportation. There was no ramp on the trailer and I had to make an awkward step up that I wasn't used to. The trailer was raw and cold inside, and it sounded like a hollow metal cave. Dried urine and manure was all over the floor mixed with moldy hay that must have been substance for other horses in my same situation. It was a wind filled fall day; gray and ominous clouds were my view through the open slats of the trailer. The cold air chilled my heart to a numb, visceral state that weakened my knees and glazed my whole body with a sense of dread. I began to shiver.

Arthur took me back to his barn where the next couple of days I was ridden by an unsophisticated barrage of riders wearing sneakers and baseball caps in the tack. They used cheap saddles that dug into my wither and forced my head into the air, causing me to gag on the cheap, dirty bits that they put in my mouth. The conditions were deplorable at best.

One girl named Cameron who worked for Arthur just seemed like a victim of her circumstance. She was actually a pretty good rider. Arthur had her get on me the fifth day I was at the farm.

"Cameron I have no idea what this thing can do. Why don't you go ahead and canter him down to a jump and see what he does," Arthur directed.

Cameron was dressed neater than the other girls, and she seemed to have a sweet way about her. She didn't have the best clothes and equipment, but I could tell that she cared about what she did have. She was a neat kid, with a naturally sweet disposition which made me want to do well for her. I did my best and jumped hard for Cameron. A little too hard though, and I jumped her loose out of the tack, renewing Arthur's level of interest in me.

"Let's go up two," he said. He repeated that statement several times, and five minutes later we were just under the four foot mark on the standards. I heard Arthur get on the phone to shop me to local barns. One trainer named Suzie took the bait that Arthur set, and she took it hard. Two days later I was sold again.

Chapter 9
The Killer Pen

Suzie didn't even bother to look in my eye when she picked me up. She was so preoccupied with the notion that she was going to be able to make money off of me that she just gave me a quick glance. She slipped Arthur the fifteen hundred dollars that he had flipped me for and loaded me on to her trailer and drove me to her stables.

My eyes took a moment to adjust as I walked into her dark, shadowy barn. I had a wonderful surprise when I was finally able to focus.

"Brielle!" I shouted when I saw my old friend in the corner stall with her nose pressed up against the stall bars.

"Bravado!" Brielle shouted back, as she ran circles around her stall.

"Settle down!" yelled Suzie, her blown out paddock boots bearing the weight of her portly stature.

Brielle ran towards the back of the stall at the sound of Suzie's reprimand. Later that night she filled me in on what was going on.

"Bravado, you have to stay in line here. This girl is not a horseman. She is just another wannabe trainer. She is constantly yelling at everyone and talking a big game to cover up for what she doesn't know."

"I don't get it Brielle, how did you end up here?"

"This barn is close to Hailey's house, and I think this Suzie fooled them into thinking she knows what she's doing. You know how it is Bravado, there are hardly any good horseman left. It is not like it used to be, but it's not all bad. Just do your best and hopefully someone nice will come through the barn and buy or lease you."

"Okay, thanks Brielle," I replied, talking with a soft concern emanating from my body language. My dear friend looked weaker than she had in the past. The atmosphere didn't help either. The old bank barn had paint chipping from the walls that mixed in with years of dust and grime. The cob webs on the stall bars made it even more difficult for me to see Brielle as she once was. I waited for daylight with circumspect, cautiously optimistic about my circumstances.

In order to get a sense of my value, Suzie and her riders jumped me hard every day for three straight days. I could feel my body getting weaker and my tendons were becoming fatigued. Suzie had no idea how to put a horse in a program. She was so ignorant to basic horse care, and my body was paying the price. The anemically bedded stall had so little sawdust that when I urinated my pee splashed all over my legs. When I tried to lie down to rest from the workouts urine and manure matted my hair, leaving large patterns of my own excrement on my body that no one bothered to wash off. It was so humiliating.

The fourth day at Suzie's I walked out of the stall crippled. They brought me back to their poor excuse for an arena. The footing was so hard it felt more like a parking lot when I trotted. With no warm up they sent me down to the jumps once more. I tried to hold it together but I was shot mentally and physically. I landed off of the first jump and immediately started to limp.

Suzie got on the phone to Arthur. "You sold me a lame horse!"

"Like hell I did," retorted Arthur, "that thing was fine when it left my barn!"

"Oh really Arthur? Suzie replied, her voice getting higher as she prepared her lie, "So how come when we jumped this thing over a few small cross rails he suddenly started to limp around my ring? You better come back and pick up this piece of garbage and you better bring me my cash too."

Suzie took her cell phone coated with ear wax and dirt and slid it back into her bra. That night I heard the terrible sound of Arthur's trailer come bouncing down the driveway, rattling like a cheap ride at a town carnival. I was back on the truck again. This time it was dark, the only light was the weak reflection of the truck brake lights working its way through the cracks in the old welds on the rusty rig.

Arthur and Suzie exchanged quick words of disdain, and I heard Arthur slap her cash back into her hand.

"You're lucky there is an auction tonight!"

"Whatever, Arthur," Suzie spewed back, cigarette smoke filling the whole of her pasty, dry mouth. "That's where you should have brought him in the first place!"

Arthur turned and jumped in his truck. They had set me loose inside the trailer, and I had to brace myself as the truck went down the driveway with no consideration of me in the back. A feeling of terror hit me as I thought of my friend back in the barn.

"Oh no Brielle! Brielle!" I cried out to her as loud as I could, the diesel exhaust from the truck filling my lungs with black smoke.

"Bravado! Where are you?" Brielle screamed in vain.

It was too late. I never got to say good bye to her.

I panicked. Kicking the trailer and turning around as fast as I could, I slammed myself into the walls with no regard to the sharp, rusty edges of the old rig. I screamed and I whinnied like I never had before; even deeper and louder then when they weaned me from my mother. By the time I got to the auction I felt like I had nothing left. My body was sore, I was emotionally distraught and I had lost all of my fight. Arthur walked me out of the trailer and into the auction. I followed Arthur into the auction barn, my head held low and my self esteem completely drained. Some of the people in the parking lot turned to look at me. They were pointing at me and whispering, probably trying to figure out what I was doing there and to determine if I was something they potentially wanted to bid on. I didn't even bother picking up my head. I thought about letting out a feint nicker to get someone's attention, but I was so spent in every way. I was completely depressed and my heart was filled with sadness. I had nothing more to say. No neighs, no knickers, no more whinnies; especially for the price of a two cent mint. I had given up on people. I had given up on life.

The auction house was bright and noisy. They had tied me up outside of the main sale barn. I heard people asking about me but Arthur chose to be a coward, and he had left me alone so there was nobody there to represent me. I heard the auctioneer sell off about forty five horses before they came over for me.

They called me a "lead in" because I had no one to ride me into the sale ring. I hung my head and cautiously walked into the arena so that I wouldn't hurt my foot any worse than it already was.

"As is boys! Smooth mouth!" I heard the auctioneer exclaim. This meant I wasn't guaranteed sound and my teeth showed my age to be well over twelve. With no papers at the sale, it was anybody's guess of how old I was. No one had called me Bravado since the therapy center, so I was nameless too.

I heard a lot of whispers in the crowd.

"Look at the brand on him," someone said, noticing the mark that was on my flank from when I was branded as a colt.

"How about that scar on the hind leg? Man that horse has been around."

"I bet he knows something," said another person on the rail. "He had to be somebody's jumper the way he is built. I wonder who would just dump him here?"

All the whispers didn't matter. When the auctioneer's hammer went down I was sold for three hundred and eighty five dollars to the man they call the "killer" buyer. At the lower level auctions there are actually contractors who purchase horses for their meat. I know it may sound a little strange coming from a horse, but these men are not all bad people. Of course I don't care for horse slaughter. However, sometimes in life it all depends on your paradigm as to how you view things. Some people are raised to see horses only as livestock; just like cattle. On the other hand, I am quick to criticize the people that dump a horse at an auction knowing full well that the horse had worked hard for people it's entire life. To me there is no way to explain that.

Regardless, that night I was no longer Bravado. I had no name. I was hip number 285, and I was just livestock.

They put me into the pen with the other horses that were bound for slaughter. Most of them looked a lot like me. They had sad, defeated looks, riddled with disappointment and resentment. Some of the younger ones had a look of terror; petrified with a realization that they never had a chance to live a full life, let alone that of a show horse.

Somebody pulled off my plain leather halter that I still had from Thompson. They replaced it with a cheap nylon halter that was too tight, causing a rope burn on my cheeks and jaw. They tied me in a small pen with about twenty other horses. After all the recent moves to different barns, the poor nutrition, strenuous work and emotional stress I had lost about two hundred pounds. I knew I looked terrible. I was lame, underweight and headed for slaughter. I had nothing left to offer anyone. So I prayed.

Chapter 10
John the Baptist

I stared blankly through the slats of the steel pen that I been moved to, overtaken by the mix of smells that I was experiencing. The odor didn't quit at the combination of damp sawdust, piling manure and gallons of urine flowing from scores of twelve hundred pound animals. Also looming in the stuffy air was over-priced hair products designed to make skanky horses look better despite not being bathed in months. Combined with the lingering stink of deep fried food, some of which was undoubtedly animal flesh, I had completely lost my appetite.

The other horses around me were speculating about what would happen next. Some overweight man wearing suspenders and waddling sideways due to his overconsumption of the aforementioned auction barn cuisine would approach me. With a palatable degree of passive aggressive tendencies he would snatch the lead rope from underneath my chin. Without a single look or sense of sympathy he would walk me straight onto the slaughter truck.

The drive that the other horses and I would endure would last hundreds of miles. No one would talk; we would just hang our heads and do our best to keep balance. Some of us would sob, while others would stare blankly outside at the passing countryside, replaying the memories of our youth in our minds, desperately looking for any form of comfort.

Then, in the closing hour of the auction I heard a promising voice from behind me.

"Look at that brand on this one. What is he doing in the kill pen?

"Forget it John," said a voice of reason, "look at his back leg. He probably won't even make it home."

"That's an old injury Nancy. That ain't going to bother him." replied John defensively, the pitch of his voice indicating he was even more interested than moments before.

"Come on, it's getting late and I want to get home. Remember, he's in the killer pen for a reason. You can't save them all."

"Just wait a minute Nance, I have a feeling about this horse."

John came around to my head and flipped my upper lip to get a look at my teeth to try and determine my age. "Yikes, he has to be about fifteen or sixteen, the poor old thing."

"Okay, great John. You don't need another horse right now. Just let him go."

"Nope, not this time Nancy. This is going to be this one's lucky night. It's clear he has worked hard for somebody, and he may have just slipped through the cracks. He doesn't deserve this fate."

"I know I am not going to change your mind when you get like this," groaned Nancy. "Fine, let's go find out who bought him at the sale and see if he will sell him to us."

I never truly knew the meaning of the word hope until I heard John's voice. He was so articulate with certainty and impassioned about his conviction that I immediately felt reassured.

The next thing I knew there were several people standing near me having a conversation like the many conversations that were had in front of my stall before. This time though, it was very different. It was as if angels and demons were fighting over my soul, deliberating over the decision on whether I was going to go to heaven or if I was going to go to hell.

After John gave a soulful, convincing speech to the slaughter agent to let me go to him, I heard the best seven words of my life.

"Fine, man. I will take fifty profit."

I was saved, at least for the moment. John loaded me on his trailer and took me to his stable. It was a warm, cozy old bank barn full of fat, happy horses. The other horses that lived there just kind of stared at me when I came through, and I could tell that they felt sorry for me. They were trying to talk to me but I had nothing to say to them. John loaded my stall up with several inches of fresh sawdust and a pile of hay to make me comfortable. I was extremely grateful for everything he was doing for me.

"I'm going up to the house John. I'm done for the night. Don't stay out too long."

"Okay Nance, got it. I love you honey. Thanks for backing me on this."

"Did I have a choice?" Nancy smiled while giving him a reassuring wink. "I love you too John. See you soon."

John stayed out in the barn for a couple hours organizing things and talking to each horse as he passed by their stall. I could tell he was a good horseman. He was an old school type. Tough, not that business smart, and a real heart for the horses. I saw pictures on the wall from the 1970's when he was a top rider. They were all in black and white, the dust creating a slight film making it hard to see the details. There was a richness about each photograph, each with a story that I was dying to hear. When John looked my way, his crystal blue eyes pulled my attention away from the wrinkles on his face that spoke of his years of experience. Beyond his eyes there was a light. That light led to a beautiful spirit of a man that had raised his entire family on income from the horse business. He had grinded hard his whole life in a business that he loved but didn't always love him back. His light overpowered all the bitterness and anger that he could have held onto, and left a man in front of me that was filled with goodness. The pictures showed it too. All the people clearly showed a love for John. You could tell he did more than just teach them how to ride and win. He was their friend, and he taught them how to live right and justly. My attention drifted away from the pictures and back to the hay pile.

I sighed deeply as I thought about my situation. I was used to people looking at me, but not in pity. I can remember going to the show ring where everyone knew my name and practically worshipped me. Now I was just a lonely, sad story of a horse saved from slaughter. No one knew my history, so it was like I was starting all over.

The next day John came out to the barn early. He decided that he needed to give me a name.

He took a piece of duct tape out and pasted it on my stall door and wrote the name 'Calebo.'

"How do you say it John? Is it Ca-lee-bo?" inquired one of John's working students.

"Yes, that's right! I am naming him after Caleb from the Old Testament. Caleb was one of the only Israelites to be brave enough to fully trust God and enter the Promised Land. I believe he is a brave horse, and I also believe that he may have a wonderful future ahead even though things may have looked bleak for him. He trusted us enough to follow us onto the trailer. So we will do our best to get him sound and healthy again."

John went right to the tasks of putting weight on me and getting me back in working condition. He had the dentist check my teeth, and he fed me very high quality hay and grain. He had a couple of teenage girls working for him who got to rubbing on my coat and who pulled my mane to a respectable and even length.

Next for me was the veterinarian. John knew that I wasn't sound, and he also knew that if I couldn't be fixed that he may need to just put me to sleep. A more respectable death than the one I was bound for, but death nonetheless.

"What did you get yourself into this time John?" his vet asked, half serious and half kidding with him at the same time.

"Let's just see what we have Doc. He isn't sound on his right front leg."

The veterinarian was very straight and to the point. I was anxious to hear what the diagnosis would be, and I did my best to behave for his procedures. They did all the routine tests that included the flexing of my legs and gauging the sensitivity of my hooves with a metal clamp called a hoof tester. They called me stoic, but the truth was that I was in a catatonic state from the sale barn experience. I was choosing to stay that way in order to emotionally and mentally protect myself.

"I think it is his coffin joint, John. Let's inject it and see what happens."

"Okay, Doc. You would know what's best."

"We'll see John, just don't get your hopes up."

"You got it, Doc. All business here" John said with his smile full of generosity and hope. "All business."

Chapter 11
Nothing More To Say

John followed the vet's protocol perfectly, like any excellent horseman would. The instructions were to keep me in a stall for three days, only to be hand walked for two of them. On day four I was allowed to be turned out in a small paddock. The first question they had to answer was whether or not the injection into my coffin joint worked to make me sound. If I looked better, they knew they had a shot at bringing me back to work. If I didn't jog sound, it could mean that it would be the end for me.

Because I had been locked up for so long, John was cautious, assuming I would be excited because of the excess energy I would be storing. I was so run down though. I barely wanted to walk, let alone act up.

"Come on Calebo!" John hollered, three small cluck sounds coming from his pursed lips as he practically jogged in place, trying to urge me along.

I had nothing to offer.

"Get up!" growled one of the barn girls as she chased me from behind with her arms flailing.

I reacted instinctively from her actions and I scooted forward, nearly stepping on John's foot.

The noise of my hooves falling on the black top echoed evenly against the backdrop of oak trees along the hedgerow. Clip-clop, clip-clop.

"Wow that looked sound to me. What did you see Nancy?"

"He looked good John. Do you want me to jog him for you?"

"Sure, just be careful Nancy."

"Got it. He looks pretty dull, I doubt he will do anything."

Just then, I remembered Nancy trying to talk John out of buying me at the sale. Feeling vengeful, when John handed the lead rope to her I pretended to spook just to scare her a little bit. I guess felt a little better than I thought. I went a little too far with it, and I jumped up in the air and spun the other way, leaving Nancy standing there empty handed.

"Oh no!" cried out Nancy. "I was afraid that might happen!"

With mixed feelings of pleasure and guilt, I jogged about twenty steps down the driveway and stopped to eat grass.

"Well, that got the job done," John said as he cautiously walked over to pick up the end of the lead rope which was precariously lying in between my front hooves, the chain shank still across my nose. "He looks good and sound to me."

The next couple days they turned me out in the small paddock near the house where John and Nancy could keep an eye on me. Then, about an hour after evening feeding John pulled me out to tack me up to see how I would be to ride. Because he got me at the auction and there was no information on me he had no idea what to expect.

John got on and just planted his hands quietly into my neck. He was very quiet with his legs and asked me to trot around the arena. When he went by Nancy and the barn girls on the rail he spoke up. "This old boy feels pretty broke!"

I could tell John was pleased, and I wished I could tell him my story, just like I wanted to hear about the pictures on his wall.

The next few months they spent riding me for short periods and jumping me over small jumps.

John eventually got me fit enough to where I could jump around a three foot course pretty handily. By way of his good horsemanship, he put the weight back on that I had lost after being shuffled around by those creeps that called themselves horsemen.

Things seemed to be turning around for the most part. John leased me out to some very nice equitation riders who showed me on the local circuits, far away from where I had shown my whole life. I ended up spending three years in John's program, knocking around the small shows and making memories with different families. Everyone on the big circuit had long forgotten about me at this point, as all the new blood from Europe had been filtering in, becoming the new Grand Prix stars of that time. I knew I was a 'has been', but it felt good to be working. Despite the opportunity to work, I still felt numb emotionally every day. There is a name for horses like me on the circuit. They are called machines. I went and did my job, and continued my vow of silence despite the love John was showing me. I would live to regret that, but I was determined to keep my mouth shut and simply take care of my business.

I still feel guilty about not being more affectionate toward John after all he had done for me. He gave me unconditional love and he had saved me from slaughter. I was so busy wallowing in self-pity that I didn't bother to do the things that I know owners love. I should have given him a nicker at night when he came out for the final evening check on the horses. I could have softly put my muzzle on him when he was going over his student's final instructions before we went into the show ring to jump our course. I didn't do anything special for him though, because I was so stuck in the past that I didn't bother to think of anyone but myself.

One night he came into my stall to adjust my blankets. He knelt down and ran his hands up and down my legs to make sure I was in good order. He then reached up to my neck, and just like a little boy saying good night to his daddy, he gave me a big hug. "Good night old boy," he said tenderly.

The next day started like any other. We all were fed and turned out to our pastures one by one to stretch our legs and graze on the hay John had left out for us. John's first training horse of the day was a two year old colt.

Nancy had told him he was getting too old for the babies, but John knew he needed to keep going to make money to pay for the farm. Nancy dreamed of retirement, but John hadn't done the best financial planning. Like many other horseman he was doing things that most sixty-seven year old men would never even consider.

That day Nancy's worst fear came true. The colt he was working with became belligerent and reared up when John was teaching him how to work on the lunge line. John was doing everything right, but somehow the lunge line got wrapped around his arm. The colt bolted and John got hung up underneath him, dragging him at a dead run around the arena. The colt panicked and accidentally trampled John, all four of his hooves making contact in a horrible array of punishing blows to the kind old man that lay lifeless underneath him. They tried to save him, but it was too late by the time one of the barn girls had found him. The ambulance came racing up the driveway to his rescue, but nothing could be done for him.

Chapter 12
The Machine

Nancy was numb. She just went through the motions of the barn work day to day completing the tasks the best that she could. She wouldn't look at me or any of the other horses. She just went up and down the barn aisle looking straight ahead with no sign of emotion. The barn girls were all so sad. It was like they had lost their own father the way they sulked with each step they took. One of the younger girls Cindy was one of John's favorite riders. She was working in the barn one day and took my water buckets out of my stall to be cleaned. John had always kept a very neat barn even though it wasn't fancy or new, and the girls wanted to make sure they honored him by maintaining his standards. She tilted the bucket sideways and started to scrub as hard as she could in a hysterical fashion, her emotions clearly taking over. She started crying uncontrollably so Nancy came over to comfort her. She put her arm around Cindy and she started to weep along with her, their tears taking two distinct paths; some falling into my water bucket while some dripped painfully onto the cold, concrete barn floor.

I wished I could comfort them somehow, but I knew there was nothing that I could do. The truth what was that I felt very guilty for not giving my best to John when he was here. I couldn't help but wonder if Nancy felt the same way. We get so busy with our lives and our own emotions and what matters to us that we don't always reach out to everybody else the way that we should. The guilt from this selfishness lingers like a disease for months, and sometimes for the rest of our lives.

Word spread that Nancy decided to scale back and lease all the horses out to other barns. She just couldn't stand looking at us because it reminded her too much of John. She thought if she leased us out that at least she would have that income to pay her bills. It was a dodgy plan, but it was her best shot at survival. Nancy was an old woman and she wasn't cut from the horseman's cloth. She had to do what whatever it took to stay afloat. I couldn't blame her, and at the same time I started to worry, because I knew this meant I was going to be heading down the road again.

John had a lot of friends in the horse business, so Nancy got on the phone and started shopping all the horses that he owned, including me. A lot of people came by to look at me, but most of them wanted me to do speed classes and it was clear I wasn't going to hold up for that. Still others weren't good enough to ride me so Nancy discouraged them from going forward.

Having all these different people try me was really difficult on me as well as Nancy, and I could tell it was wearing on her as she tried to get all of John's affairs in order. That all stopped one day when a girl named Mary came to the barn. Mary was the most energetic human that I had ever met. When she walked, she seemed to bounce with each step. The blond ponytail that she had pulled through her baseball cap swung side to side with each step that she took, and she talked so fast that I couldn't keep up with her thought process. She lit up the barn with her good nature and her positive energy.

After a brief talk, Nancy and Mary agreed that I may suit Mary's rider Tabitha.

"Are you sure this horse will be able to do the show hunters and equitation, Nancy?" Mary asked.

"I just want to make sure he is not too much because he is so big. Tabitha is coming off of a large pony and I don't want to over face her."

"You don't need to worry about this horse Mary. He's a machine."

Tabitha climbed into the tack to try me out. At the time, she just seemed like another teenage kid to me. She rode okay. She was soft handed and non-invasive. I could tell that she had gotten solid training from Mary, as she stayed very balanced in the tack. I was a little worried that I might be too much for her once we got on course. At the time I was very bitter and had no real desire to please, and I was certain I wasn't going to get emotionally vested in another human ever again. I knew I was just a lease for a year so Tabitha could accomplish her goals of getting to the equitation finals. I felt like I was just a prop for her to win and for Mary to get better clients. I was what they said I was. I was a machine.

"Everything looks good to me Nancy. Is there anything you don't like about Calebo? Does he have any vices at all?"

"Well yes, but it's not really a vice, more of a quirk. John said that he never makes a sound."

"What do you mean?" asked Mary, concerned but not alarmed.

"Just what I said. Never a whinny, a nicker or a neigh. He is completely silent. He just puts his head down and does his job."

I arrived at Mary's barn that night exhausted from the travel. I could tell the other horses were impressed by me as I walked down the barn aisle. John had managed to get me back into good shape, so at the very least I was respectable to look at. Mary and Tabitha were excited to show me off. I really didn't expect the treatment that they were giving me. I really thought they were going to treat me like a tool, rather than a horse. Despite their enthusiasm I was reluctant to let my guard down. I had moved so many times and had been let down so often that I was not ready to be vulnerable by trusting another human.

The best part about Mary's barn was the bedding. It had been almost twenty years since I was bedded on straw. The first night a rush of memories came back into my mind. I could see my Mother standing over me, the smell of the straw mixing divinely with her warm touch. That night for the first time since the auction I said a prayer, and I thanked God for sending me Mary.

I went to work the next day. Sometimes when you let people determine who you are by listening to what they say, you become what they think you are. So I went to work as the machine. I was very depressed and it caused me to be irritable. Every mistake that Tabitha made annoyed me, and I let her know about it by rushing the jumps and acting up on the cross ties. Sometimes I would take off after the jumps or leave out a stride in a line of jumps just to intimidate her. She actually handled it pretty well. Looking back I am ashamed of my behavior. I remember my backwards and selfish thinking. If I wasn't happy I didn't want anyone else to be happy either. I did just enough to get the job done so they would keep feeding me. We would go to the shows, and we would always place in the middle of the ribbons, usually fourth or fifth. This was starting to wear on Mary a little because she wanted Tabitha to qualify for finals, and at the rate we were going it wasn't going to happen.

Life on Mary's farm, Hopewell Ridge, was actually really good. There was a man named Ben who did the stalls and took care of a lot of the maintenance for Mary. He always had such a good attitude and a lot of common sense, which often times is a rarity in the horse business. He was an older man, very sensitive, and he always handled me so gently. All of the people that worked at the barn were well trained by Mary, and despite her kind demeanor and her evident youth everyone respected her. She had a great family too. Her dad, mom and her husband were so supportive and always helped her around the farm. The barn was always very busy. Between Mary and her assistant instructor Lucy there were over fifty people per week taking lessons. All the kids wanted to be just like Mary, and some of them even talked just like her. In all of my years I had never seen a barn like Hopewell Ridge. Superior horsemanship combined with a loving atmosphere made for a wonderful environment.

Mary was always such a joy to be around. She would zip up and down the barn aisle handling her chores with enthusiasm, and she would take such good care of the horses. I knew that John would have approved of my new home. I became very good friends with Mary's own personal horse Pearl. Pearl was just a couple of stalls down and across the aisle from me. She was a jokester of a horse and she always liked to interact with people and try and make them laugh. People could sense that Pearl knew what she was doing, and everyone loved her. She was actually very similar to Mary. Full of piss and vinegar, she always had a kind word for everyone around her. Pearl was very encouraging to me, and she started to talk sense into me as my time went on at Hopewell Ridge.

"You have to start being better to Tabitha," Pearl told me one spring night. She is such a kind, sweet girl and she deserves a good ride."

"You don't know what I have been through Pearl. I am just sick of being let down and being hurt."

"You are right Calebo, I don't know what you have been through, but everyone has been through something. Nobody's life is perfect. We have to be grateful for the here and now. Our past is just the past, and we have no reason but to have hope for the future."

"I suppose you are right," I replied to Pearl.

"I know I am right Calebo. Now you have to pull yourself together and start showing your faith."

"I'll do my best Pearl."

Pearl's advice reminded me so much of my mother's advice so many years ago.

One morning Mary and Tabitha were talking outside my stall. Tabitha was getting discouraged about our progress. "I just don't get him Mary. I try so hard to ride my best but we just can't get in sync."

"You just have to keep at it Tabitha. You have to be persistent."

"I know Mary, I am just afraid that my parents will not want to pay for Calebo's lease anymore if we don't get our act together."

"You can't think that way, Tabitha. Your parents are very supportive and they just want what is best for you."

"You have three more shows to get ready for the Gateway series up north. You will get it together."

I picked my head up sharply from my hay. I couldn't believe what Mary had just said. We were going to the Gateway show series. I hadn't been to that show for years. If I made it there I might see some of my old friends.

"Okay Mary, I will make sure I do extra work without my stirrups this week."

"That's the spirit, Tabitha!" Mary screeched, her high, happy voice resonating joy throughout the whole barn.

I started to get a little bit excited at the thought of being able to see some of my old friends. I decided to put in a better effort at the next few shows. The trouble was that I had been mediocre on purpose for so long I actually was getting good at being sub par. I had to get sharper for Gateway and I knew it. To complicate things further I could tell that Tabitha was starting to feel pressure to perform well, and she was talking about how she was feeling pressure from school as well. I started to worry about her, but at least I was getting my head straight. I just couldn't shake the depression, but I took Pearl's advice and I dug in. As Gateway approached I prayed for strength to be my best and to find my happiness again. Pearl was right, I needed to have faith, and I had to do my best to help Tabitha. This wasn't about me. It never was.

Chapter 13
Best Show Ever

It was a warm spring day, the kind where the footing gave just the right amount underneath my feet and the air was only chilly enough to keep us from sweating.

Mary had brought fifteen of us to Gateway to compete, and we got settled into the show stables quickly. We were loaded up on hay and bedding, just like at home. Tabitha was excited and so was I. She took me out of my stall to go to one of the warm up rings. I looked around but I didn't see any of my old friends, and I started to get a little concerned. I started thinking that maybe it had been so long that they were all gone or retired.

I went into machine mode as Tabitha started trotting me around the ring. My nickname for her was 'kind sweet girl'. She was always so particular about everything. Her boots were perfectly polished, and her hair net draped neatly across her ear, a small pearl earring reserved for horse show days glistening on her petite ear lobe. She was careful not to wear too much bling so that it wouldn't distract from the beauty of the horse, and she was always respectful to her parents as well as Mary.

As we warmed up in the schooling ring, suddenly I started to hear a lot of people chatter. There were people pointing and whispering at me. I didn't think much about it at first but then more and more people kept giving me weird looks. I could tell Mary was getting annoyed and actually a little bit freaked out with everyone pointing at me.

I couldn't believe what I saw next. It was Tim! He approached Mary aggressively, and I could see Mary was on the defensive.

"How did you get that horse?" Tim asked, partially excited to see me, partially angry that it was at a horse show.

"What do you mean?" asked Mary, her voice already elevated. "I leased him from John and Nancy Goodman's down south."

"Nobody is supposed to have that horse. I retired him from showing years ago to a therapeutic riding center when Babylon went under."

"You must have him confused with another horse," Mary said dismissively. "This is Calebo. I am telling you I leased him from Nancy after John had passed away."

"You can call him whatever you want, but there is only one horse in the world with that brand and that scar," Tim said confidently as he took his phone out of his back pocket. He handed Mary his phone to show her a picture of me at the last Grand Prix Tim and I did together. Just as Mary's jaw started to drop my old groom Carlos came over smiling and pointing at me.

"Bravado! Bravado!" He kept saying over and over again, his Spanish accent rolling the r in my name, causing everyone in the schooling ring to stop and stare right at Mary and Tim.

"Bravado?" Mary said, her voice taking on an acquiescing tone. "*The* Bravado? The Grand Prix horse?"

"I think we need to chat a bit to get this sorted out," Tim said.

"I suppose so," Mary said, her cheeks the color of red wine. "Tabitha, take Calebo, umm, Bravado-whatever, just go stretch him out okay honey?"

Tabitha and I went back to hacking while Tim and Mary retraced my history.

"Arthur was involved with this? He just can't help himself, can he? I can't believe he weaseled his way into that therapy center and then had the nerve to dump him at the sale. Boy do I owe John and Nancy for saving him. I wish I had gone to his funeral. Man I feel terrible," his voice trailed off.

"How did you not know about all this Tim?"

"When Babylon went under and they dispersed the horses I couldn't handle it. I got out of the business all together and went back to finish my MBA. I actually just got back into the game about six months ago. I am really glad you ended up with him Mary. Your reputation precedes you."

"Thanks Tim, that is very gracious of you, especially after I just blasted you in the schooling ring in front of everybody. I am really sorry about that."

"Oh my goodness Mary, you don't need to apologize. I am sorry too. Hey, you are not going to believe this, but I actually have one of Calebo's babies from when he was a stallion."

"Seriously?"

"Yes, how would you like to meet him?"

"Oh my gosh, are you kidding me? Yes! Please!"

Tim got out his phone and called back to one of his grooms in the barn. "Hey Kim, bring Whiskers up to the ring. There is somebody here that wants to meet him. As a matter of fact, tack him up so I can ride him for our new friends."

I had caught bits and pieces of the conversation, but the wind was passing through my ears and I figured I was just imagining things. Then suddenly I saw a sight more beautiful than anything that I had ever seen before.

"Whiskers! Whiskers!" I screamed. The whole show grounds went silent as my whinny echoed throughout the riding rings and the barns.

"Daddy! Daddy!" Whiskers screamed back.

"I can't believe it. Calebo is whinnying!" Mary exclaimed.

I started prancing in place and I could feel Tabitha start to tense up, unsure of how to handle me. Without even thinking, I did my trademark step where I placed my foot carefully well out in front of my regular foot pattern, extending my hoof softly down to the ground in front of me. They led Whiskers over to me and we touched our noses together. We both squealed with excitement. They quietly separated us, and Tim got a leg up on Whiskers. For the first time in my life, my son and I rode off together in the same ring.

The horse show was buzzing with the story. I had found a whole new level of energy and my heart was overflowing with happiness. I couldn't wait for my chance to compete, and I felt like there was no way anyone could beat me. I knew I had to give my confidence to Tabitha. I remembered how anxious she was about this show, and I wanted to make her feel special this week. I was so grateful to God for what he had done for me, and I swore that I would do my best to never let anyone down again.

Tabitha and I won our division handily the next day, and our success continued over the weekend in her big class. With every jump she pointed me at I patiently waited for her cues, and I jumped harder and more beautiful than I had in years. Tabitha was terrific, and her parents were so happy for her.

That's how it went for the rest of the summer. With my renewed sense of purpose, Tabitha and I became the team to beat. My whinny was back, and each morning I was so excited to see Mary come down the barn aisle, her pony tail swinging side to side as she happily dumped our morning grain into our feed bins.

Just before finals Mary came down the barn aisle, her normal chipper self. I overheard her on the phone giving someone directions to the farm. Mary had gotten a new student, and she was bringing her horse to the barn that day. I heard the trailer pull up and the truck door slam. Right away I recognized the voice of the girl speaking with Mary, but I couldn't place it. Then I spun around in my stall in a fury of excitement at the words that came out of the girl's mouth.

"This is my mare. Her name is Brielle. Where would you like her to go?"

"There is a stall open next to the black horse on the end," Mary said as she pointed in my direction. "You will see it, his name plate says Calebo."

I yelled as loud as I could for Brielle.

"Bravado, is that really you?" Brielle whinnied back, her voice echoing through the whole barn.

"I am so sorry Mary," Hailey said, "she is never like this."

"I am sure she is just excited to be at a new place. She will settle down," Mary said reassuringly.

"Yes, it's me!" I whinnied back.

Mary raced down to my stall to check on me. "Calm down Calebo, you're acting like you are still a stallion. I wonder what got into him?"

"Oh my gosh!" exclaimed Hailey. "Is that really him? Calebo?"

"Yes, that is our boy," Mary said proudly.

"I heard the story on social media," said Hailey with excitement in her young voice. "I am sure Brielle will be glad to see him. They were stable mates a long time ago when he was known as Bravado."

"Oh my goodness!" exclaimed Mary. "Really? What a small world! They must be so happy to see each other."

Mary and Hailey looked on as Brielle and I reached out over our stall guards to look at each other, our eyes wild with bliss at our fate.

"Do you think they can get turned out together?" Hailey asked Mary.

"I don't usually turn mares out with geldings, but I think I can make an exception in this case. They seem so happy to see each other. I think it would break their hearts if I didn't keep them together."

I filled Brielle in on my name change, and explained to her everything that I had been through. Afraid to make her worry though, I didn't tell her everything that I knew. Tabitha's finals were coming and afterwards my lease would be up. That meant I may have to go to a different barn to be leased out by someone else. I was taking Pearl's advice and I was staying in the moment. I was praying too, praying that somehow I would stay with Mary at Hopewell Ridge for the rest of my life.

Chapter 14
Ponytail Angel

Finals came, and Tabitha and I took care of business. She rode really terrific and we ended up at the top of the class. Back at the barn that night everybody seemed really happy. My whole team was sitting outside of my stall in lawn chairs going over the details of our class and saying how wonderful it was. Then someone spoke up and killed the moment when they mentioned something about me going back to Nancy's or to another barn since the lease was up. They pointed out Tabitha was going to college, and Mary didn't have anyone lined up for me.

That night I didn't sleep much. I felt desperate, and I was clinging to my faith for strength. Often times when I would get sad I would talk to my mom in heaven. I talked to her that night and I also prayed to God for a miracle. I had declared the desire of my heart years ago was to spend my final days side by side with Brielle. Now even though it seemed so close to happening I knew it could be taken away from me any day.

"Please God," I prayed, "change the situation and help Mary somehow keep me forever. Forgive me for all of the wrong that I have ever done and when I let you down. I am so sorry for not being my best all the time, just please grant me this request." I hoped with all of my heart that my prayers would be answered.

Tabitha had tucked me into my stall neatly for the night. I had a sheet on to keep me warm, and all four of my legs were wrapped with quilts to keep the blood circulating to my tendons. Standing over a huge pile of hay that Mary had generously given me, I fell fast asleep.

The next morning I woke up to the sound of Mary's cell phone ringing.

"Yes, yes, okay, okay, great. Thank you! Thank you! Yes, that'll work. Okay great," Mary chimed quickly, her voice getting faster with each word that she spoke.

She was too far away so I couldn't hear the other person on the phone. I assumed it was a lesson mom scheduling her child for the week.

Mary was always so happy-even about everyday things that it was sometimes hard to tell what she was thinking. She went to the feed room and started dishing out the morning feed to all the horses. When she got to me she reached her hand in her pocket and laid a handful of peppermints on top of my food bucket.

Always happy to see extra peppermints I looked up at her and gave her a quick nod of thanks.

"Well Calebo, I got some news for you buddy. It looks like you and me are in it for the long haul."

I took my nose and I slammed the feed bucket against the stall wall as hard as I could to try and force more details out of her. The feed flew all over Mary, and she squealed and giggled like a ten year old girl as she brushed herself off.

"Easy boy!" she smiled. "You are staying here. You are all mine now!"

I ran circles around my stall and snaked my neck in excited approval. Brielle stomped and nickered with glee. Tabitha came walking down the barn aisle, her saddle propped up on her hip with her right arm, her other arm free by her side.

"Tabitha you won't believe it. Nancy called me this morning and offered to give me Calebo."

Tabitha's eyes widened with excitement at the news. Mary's voice became higher and higher with each word that she spoke to Tabitha, causing all the horses to pick their heads up from their morning hay and fix their eyes on Mary.

"Things have really turned around for her financially and she said that when she woke up this morning she felt led by her heart to call me and offer him to me."

"That's amazing!" Tabitha put her saddle down on the closest rack and grabbed Mary and gave her a big hug. I am so happy for you Mary! I am so happy for Calebo too!"

"I didn't want to say anything, but deep down I was hoping for this the whole time. My parents and Mark were so supportive when they heard the news. I am so grateful to have such amazing parents and an incredible husband."

"What are you planning to do with him? Are you going to lease him out again?"

"Nope, he is going to stay right here at Hopewell Ridge for the rest of his life. We can use him in lessons to teach the younger kids the ropes, and keep going to the shows as long as he seems happy doing it. Heaven knows he deserves it after what he has been through. Besides, I could never take him from Brielle. They just seem so happy together."

"A horse like this who has touched so many people and accomplished so many amazing things deserves the absolute best until his last days."

A few of the barn girls and Tabitha all gathered around my stall as Mary spoke. They listened intently, sensing that Mary was about to give them one of her valuable life lessons.

"Girls, it is so vital for you to remember to look around and appreciate all of the amazing people in your life everyday that love you and care about you. Staying in a state of gratitude will give you strength. Just think for a minute about what Calebo has been through. He spent his entire life giving himself completely to others. Despite his sometimes terrible circumstances he always persevered. His tenacity is a characteristic we need to emulate when we start to get down on ourselves. We always have to believe for the best, because no matter what happens to us our faith will always carry us through. Everything will always work out."

The girls left the barn, leaving just me and Mary in the stable. The only sound I could hear was the rest of the horses quietly chewing their hay. I could tell that despite her outward happiness,

Mary was exhausted inside from all of her hard work. Like a lot of people she had been through many hard times in her life. Mary and I had quietly bonded through my year at Hopewell Ridge. We had that rare, wonderful type of relationship where two people understand each other without having to say anything at all.

"I need to thank you Calebo. Thank you for everything that you have done for me and for everyone else you ever touched. You are such a special horse, and I am so grateful for you."

I lowered my head and softened my eye, reflecting back my heartfelt gratitude to Mary for all she had done for me as well.

Mary looked at me affectionately as she gently opened my stall door, but her usual smile ran away from her face as she opened her arms to me. I came to her and dropped my head towards her chest as she laid her head against mine. Mary shed a tear which dripped off of her cheek and joined one of my own tears in mid air, falling as one perfect tear drop onto the golden bed of straw beneath us.

Whether you turn to the right or the left, your ears will hear a voice behind you saying, "This is the way; walk in it."
~Isaiah 30:21

GRATITUDE AND A WORD ABOUT SELF-PUBLISHING

Thank you for reading *Horse Gone Silent*. I hope that Calebo's story touched your heart in a special way. If you did enjoy my work, I really need your help to spread the word to other people. When you share with people and review on sites like Amazon.com, this has a *profound* effect on the success of a self-publisher like me. You really can make a difference. Thank you so much for your wonderful support.

"Stay strong and courageous!"

Connect with me and find out about future novels and other work at www.HorseGoneSilent.com.

ABOUT THE AUTHOR

Shane Ledyard is a classic American horseman who brings the intrigue and lure of the horse world alive in "Horse Gone Silent". Raised in old school horse country, he has been influenced by a colored past involving horse shows over many parts of the country, horse auctions and the race tracks. He makes his living in the horse business as a rider, trainer, judge and instructor. When he is not working with the horses he is spending his time loving his beautiful wife Carice and his children Kevin and Kaydy.

Made in the USA
San Bernardino, CA
04 March 2017